The Adventures of
Pinky and Bluey

The Fire Truck

Nic & Lauren Reader

Pinky and Bluey
Copyright © 2024 by Nic & Lauren Reader

All rights reserved. No part of this publication may be reproduced, distributed, or transmitted in any form or by any means, including photocopying, recording, or other electronic or mechanical methods, without the prior written permission of the author, except in the case of brief quotations embodied in critical reviews and certain other non-commercial uses permitted by copyright law.

Tellwell Talent
www.tellwell.ca

ISBN
978-1-77941-862-3 (Hardcover)
978-1-77941-861-6 (Paperback)
978-1-77941-863-0 (eBook)

Dedication

To my grandma, Francis, and my dad, Rick, for creating this wonderful world and sharing their beautiful imagination.

Acknowledgments

Pinky and Bluey's adventures have been told through four generations, and we are thrilled to now share them with you.

This is the story of Pinky and Bluey.

Pinky wears a pink hat and a pink coat.

Bluey wears a blue hat and a blue coat.

Pinky and Bluey are twins who look similar on the outside but are very different on the inside.

One morning, Pinky and Bluey are finishing their breakfast when they hear a fire truck siren coming up the road. The two race to the window, wondering where it might be heading.

The pigs watch the fire truck until it is gone, and the sounds of the siren trail off.

Pinky looks at Bluey and asks, "What should we do today?"

As Bluey thinks, he gets an idea!

"Let's build our own fire truck!" Bluey yells excitedly.

"Oh! We can paint it red and race it down the Big Hill," Pinky says, always up for an adventure.

The two pigs jump from the windowsill and run outside.

They pass Papa, who is working on the tractor.

"What are you two up to this morning?" Papa asks.

Bluey tells Papa all about the fire truck and how they want to build their own. Looking at the two pigs, Papa laughs and tells them to use anything in the barn.

Pinky and Bluey open the barn door and look in. There are bins, tool boxes, old tractor parts, and odds and ends of all kinds. Pinky spots a large cardboard box in the corner.

"There." Pinky points.

The twins rush over and pull the box out.
Bluey hands Pinky a can of red paint and
a brush as he looks for more parts.

Pinky paints the box bright red. She uses
scissors to make the perfect window cutouts
just as Bluey pulls an old red wagon around.

"This will make a perfect frame and wheels," he says.

Pinky and Bluey put the box on the wagon. Pinky
finds a cowbell hiding behind a bin; she ties it to
the box with twine and gives it a little ding-ding.

The fire truck is almost complete. Pinky looks
everywhere and spots an old steering wheel
sticking out from a shelf. She climbs up and
grabs it, tossing it down to Bluey. They attach
it to the wagon handle, and they're all set.

"To the Big Hill!" Pinky yells.

The pigs push their new fire truck
out of the garage past Papa.

"Wait a second, you two," he says. "A fire truck needs a fire hose, right?" Papa reaches down and lifts an old garden hose. He helps Pinky tie it to the side of the fire truck, pats the truck, and tells them, "Have fun."

The pigs reach the bottom of the Big Hill, and Bluey looks up, worried.

"This thing isn't going to push itself to the top," Pinky says.

Pinky and Bluey start pushing and pulling their fire truck up the side of the hill. It gets steeper and steeper, but the pigs keep going.

"Come on, Bluey, almost there," Pinky grunts.

The pigs finally reach the very top, and now they stand looking at their fire truck. It's perfect: bright red with a shiny cowbell flashing in the sun.

Bluey looks at Pinky. "I'll drive," he says.

With Bluey in the driver's seat, Pinky pretends to get an emergency call.

Pinky holds up her hand like a phone and answers, "Hello, this is the Fire Department. Oh, there's a fire at Mr. Chicken's house? We are on our way!" She looks at her brother and says, "There's a fire at Mr. Chicken's; let's go!"

Pinky pushes the truck toward the edge of the hill.

The fire truck creeps toward the slope and starts to roll down. The twins squeal with excitement as the fire truck picks up speed. It rolls faster and faster. Bluey's smile disappears as he tries to steer. Pinky and Bluey hold on as the fire truck picks up more speed.

As they rocket down the hill, the fire truck is going so fast that the pigs wonder how they will stop. Bluey yells, "We forgot brakes." Pinky rings the cowbell, calling for help: Ding, Ding, Ding, "Help!"

The fire truck reaches the bottom of the Big Hill but starts to climb the next slope. It slows down a little as it reaches the top.

The pigs are relieved as they come to a stop. But suddenly, the fire truck starts to roll backward. They yell for help while the truck picks up speed again.

Pinky grabs the garden hose and tosses it toward a tree. Like an anchor, the hose wraps around the trunk and helps the fire truck stop near the bottom of the hill. Pinky and Bluey jump out of the fire truck just as Mama and Papa come running.

"That was a close one!" Bluey says.

"That was awesome!" Pinky yells.

Mama and Papa pick them up to see if they're ok.

"Maybe next time, make sure it can stop," Papa says.

The twins laugh nervously and start to push their fire truck back home.

"Maybe it's time to add brakes," Pinky says.

About the Authors

Nic and Lauren Reader are married and have three children. Lauren earned her master's degree in education, and Nic is a creative director in the film and television industry. They love creating, making, and sharing things with friends and family.

Printed in the USA
CPSIA information can be obtained
at www.ICGtesting.com
LVHW071746051224
798427LV00036B/550